A Boy Wants A Dinosaur

Hiawyn Oram
Satoshi Kitamura

ANDERSEN PRESS
LONDON

Ben had a dog.
Alice had two snails.
Alex wanted a dinosaur.

He lay on his bed and sobbed and cried.
"But I want a dinosaur," he sobbed, "a dinosaur is
what I want." Until his grandfather put down his
saxophone, put on his hat and coat and said,
"A boy wants a dinosaur this much, a boy should
have a dinosaur…"

…and took him to the Dino-Store. The Dino-Store was big and glassy. It took up most of Ginkgo Street. For someone who wanted a dinosaur it was certainly the place to be.

On the ground floor were the grown dinosaurs. On the first floor were the young dinosaurs. In the basement the baby Hadrosaurus splashed in the Hadrosaurium.

On the top floor the Pterosaurs soared in the Pterosaviary and on the second floor there was everything you could ever need for a dinosaur.

First Alex thought he wanted a Triceratops. Then he thought he
wanted a Fabrosaur. Then, just as he had almost decided on a
Diplodocus he saw the Massospondylus and the Massospondylus
saw him

and came over and rolled on its back and rolled its eyes and licked
Alex's hand.
"I'll call him Fred," said Alex.
"But she's a girl," said his grandfather reading the sign, "a girl who
eats anything, meat and plants!"
"Then I'll call her The One Who Eats Everything, but Fred for
short," said Alex and they ordered what she would need, put on her
collar and lead and set off for home.

When they got home Alex could not wait to see Fred eat…two bags of fossils soaked in all the milk in the fridge, one drum of dried clubmoss tree, three sacks of pine needles, the washing, the neighbour's marrows and a bite out of the next-door-but-one's cat.
"Alex!" said his mother. "This is really too much!"
But Alex would not listen. "Not for a dinosaur," he said. "For a dinosaur it is only a snack…"

And he dashed upstairs, ran a steaming hot bath, added some Instant Marsh Powder and put Fred in for a good long soak.

"Alex," called his father, coming in from work, "a marsh in the house is quite unhealthy!"

"Not for a dinosaur," Alex replied crossly. "For a dinosaur it is perfectly natural..."

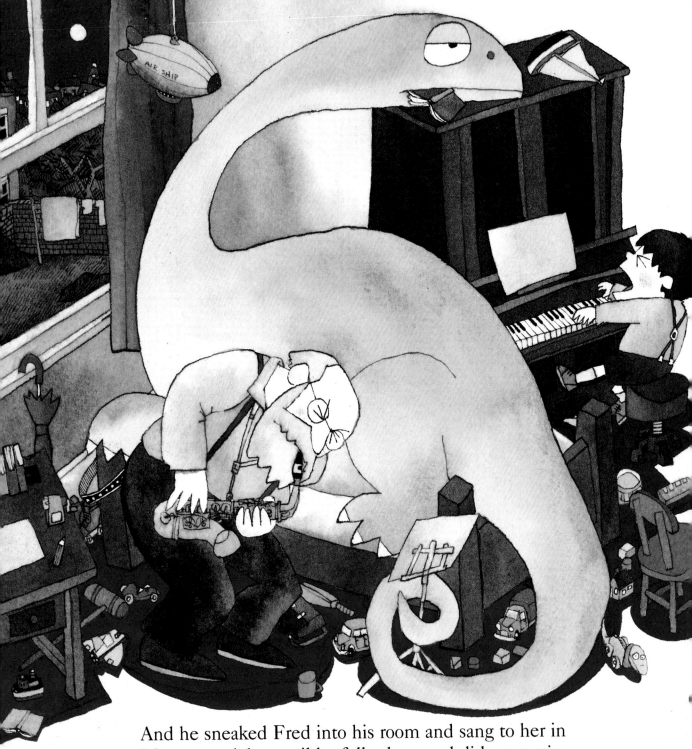

And he sneaked Fred into his room and sang to her in
Massospondylus until he fell asleep and did not notice
that she couldn't settle and chewed everything she could
find in the dark to comfort her.

When Alex's mother came in in the morning she threw her hands in the air and sat on the bedstump and wailed and cried.

"But it's terrible," she wailed, "monstrous and prehistoric!"

"Not for a dinosaur," Alex explained as patiently as he could. "For a dinosaur it's much more like home…"

And he dressed and put on Fred's collar and lead and set off for school. On the way Fred spotted a lorry turning a corner and bounded into the road and lashed out.

The lorry driver was furious. "Do you mind!" he yelled.
"This is my company's best lorry!"
"Not to my dinosaur," Alex yelled back, losing his temper.
"To my dinosaur it's probably a Tyrannosaurus Rex!"

And he dragged Fred away and into school. Alex's friends were very excited about having a dinosaur in Pets Corner but Miss Jenkins was not so sure.

"A classroom is a place for sitting still, for listening and learning with no distractions," she said.

"Not for my dinosaur," said Alex. "This classroom is making her feel very, very sick."

And he ran and got his grandfather and they took Fred to the vet.
The vet looked at Fred's tongue and listened to her heart and shone
a light into her eyes. He asked about the fight with the lorry and
X-rayed her for broken bones.
"Well?" breathed Alex. "What is it? What's the matter with her?"
"Nothing that a nice long walk in the country won't cure,"
said the vet.

And there amongst the fields of sheep and barns of hay
Fred perked up. She gambolled and lolloped, lumbered
and strode and would not stop until they reached the other
side of a thick pine forest.

Running after her, Alex saw why. Stretching all around them was a crusty old swamp edged by giant clubmoss trees. Fred reared up and ran for it.

"Now, Fred!" yelled Alex. "This is going too far!"

"NOT FOR A DINOSAUR!" shouted Alex's grandfather and with a bubbling-under shout…

…Alex woke up. For a while he lay in his unchewed
bed under his unchewed bedclothes and thought about
his dreams of a dinosaur.
Then he called his grandfather.
"Yip," said his grandfather.
"When we get a pet, I think we should get…"
"A rabbit?" said his grandfather…

"Exactly," said Alex. "And we won't call her Fred either," he sighed.